# MELVIN
## THE HAIRY FROG

by
**Ram Gulrajani**

Dedicated to Heath, Cas, Eli
Daisy, Niamh and Maeve.

Love you lots!

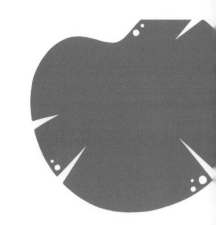

# MELVIN
## THE HAIRY FROG

by

Ram Gulrajani

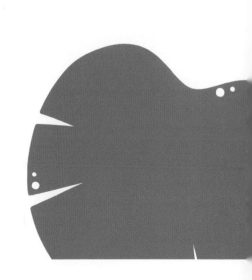

In the marsh
where Melvin dwelled,
cruel laughter
often swelled.

They'd point and mock,
'What a sight!',
his shaggy form
in the sunlight.

"No sleek skin,"
they'd snicker and jeer,
"At your odd hair,
we cannot steer clear."

"Why can't you be
like us, so neat?
Your hair's so long,
it covers your feet."

So as days passed
in the lively marsh,
the sunny weather being
far from harsh,

frogs danced and sang,
in delight and glee,
but winter was coming,
as they soon would see.

The first frost arrived,
the marsh was chilled,
the joyous chatter
quickly stilled.

Frogs shivered,
their skin turning blue,
winter was harsh,
as they well knew.

Except for Melvin,
who felt just right,
his hair kept him warm
throughout the night.

He saw his friends,
so cold, so frail,
their suffering told
a woeful tale.

So he thought hard,
what could he do?
Then an idea struck,
and off it flew.


He trimmed his hair,
keeping just enough,
this wasn't easy,
this wasn't bluff.

He weaved the hair
into tiny blankets,
cozy and warm
as little trinkets.

One by one, he gifted
them to his friends,
their gratitude,
a means to an end.

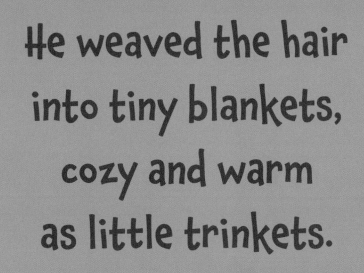

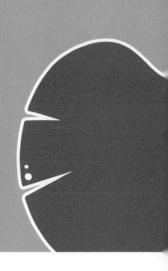

All through winter,
Melvin shared his warmth,
His hair, a gift of
immeasurable worth.

He made sure no frog
felt the winter's sting,
his kindness making
their hearts sing.

As winter passed
and spring took its course,
the frogs realized
Melvin's resource.

They thanked him,
their eyes brimming with tears,
Melvin had chased away
their winter fears.

His hair,
once a subject of jest,
Had proved to be
their survival's crest.

Melvin smiled,
feeling joy and pride,
His uniqueness had
turned the tide.

From then on,
in the marsh so grand,
Melvin was known
as the warmest hand.

His hair was celebrated,
far and wide,
he was their hero,
their hearts' guide.

And thus,
Melvin learned and taught,
that being unique
was not for naught.

In your differences,
there's strength untold,
like Melvin the hairy,
hero brave and bold.

# About the author!

This is Ram's second illustrated children's book and hopefully there will be more to follow. Enjoy this story with your little people!

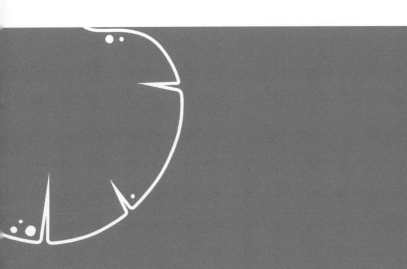

# The aim of this book

The story aims to primarily entertain and allow time between younger readers and their adult.

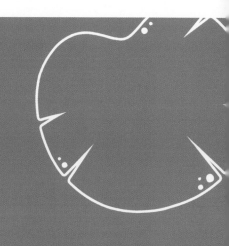

To also encourage questions and enable the younger readerto explore acceptance. Acceptnce of everyone irrespetive of how they look.

We are all different and we all have a purpose, a need for sharing and love.

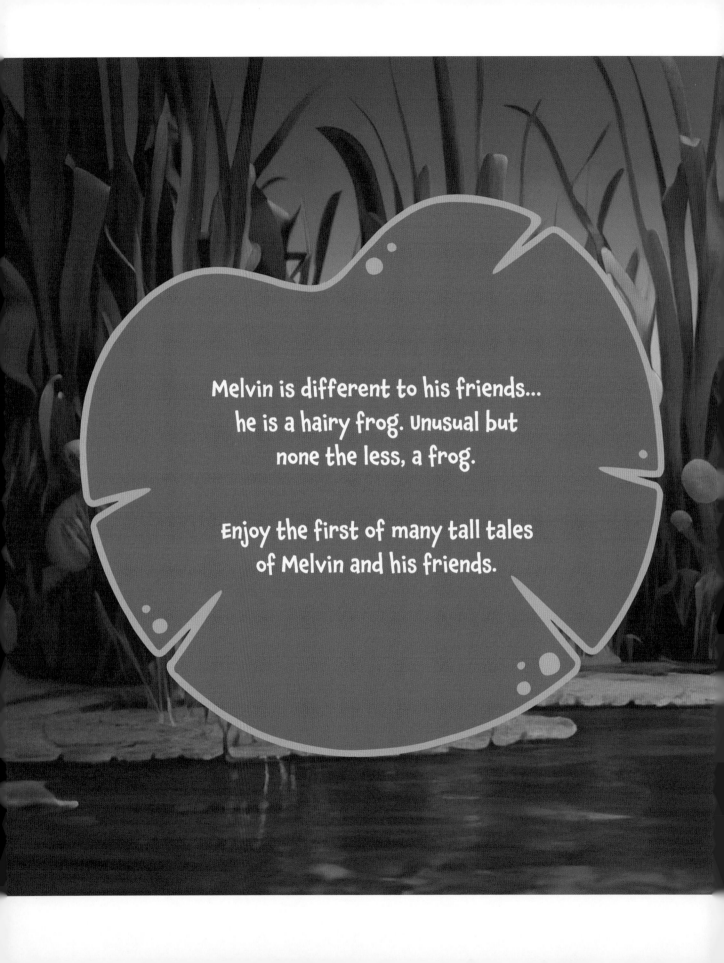

Melvin is different to his friends...
he is a hairy frog. Unusual but
none the less, a frog.

Enjoy the first of many tall tales
of Melvin and his friends.

Printed in Great Britain
by Amazon

40338566R00023